W9-BMA-197

IN THE NIGHT KITCHEN

MAURICE SENDAK

A TRUMPET CLUB SPECIAL EDITION

Published by
The Trumpet Club
666 Fifth Avenue
New York, New York 10103

Copyright © 1970 by Maurice Sendak

All rights reserved. No part of this book may be reproduced or transmitted in
any form or by any means, electronic or mechanical, including photocopying,
recording or by any information storage and retrieval system, without the written
permission of the Publisher, except where permitted by law. For information
address: Harper & Row, Publishers, Inc., New York, New York.

The Trademark Dell® is registered in the U.S. Patent and Trademark Office.
ISBN: 0-440-84730-3

Reprinted by arrangement with Harper & Row, Publishers, Inc.
Printed in the United States of America
November 1988

10 9 8 7 6 5 4 3 2

FOR SADIE AND PHILIP

DID YOU EVER HEAR OF MICKEY,
HOW HE HEARD A RACKET IN THE NIGHT

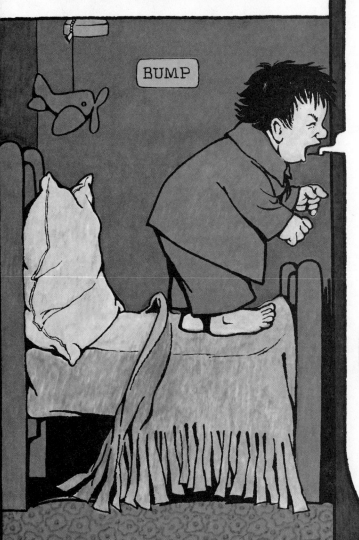

AND THEY PUT THAT BATTER UP TO BAKE

A DELICIOUS MICKEY-CAKE.

BUT RIGHT IN THE MIDDLE
OF THE STEAMING
AND THE MAKING
AND THE SMELLING
AND THE BAKING
MICKEY POKED THROUGH
AND SAID:

SO HE SKIPPED FROM THE OVEN & INTO BREAD DOUGH ALL READY TO RISE IN THE NIGHT KITCHEN.

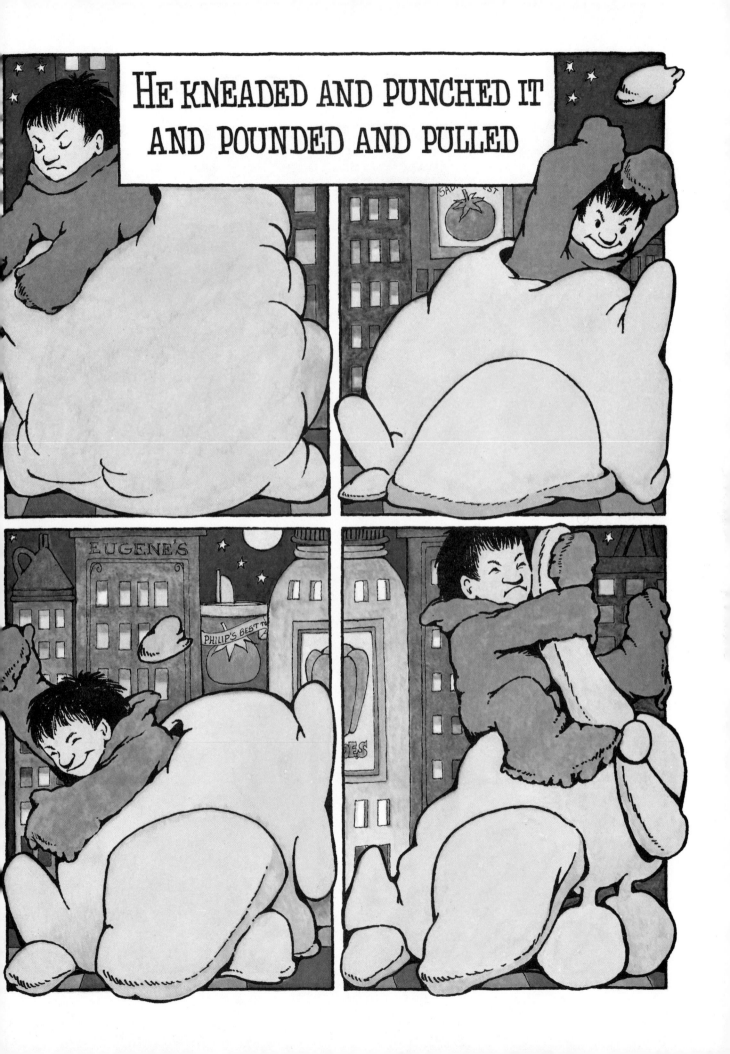

HE KNEADED AND PUNCHED IT
AND POUNDED AND PULLED

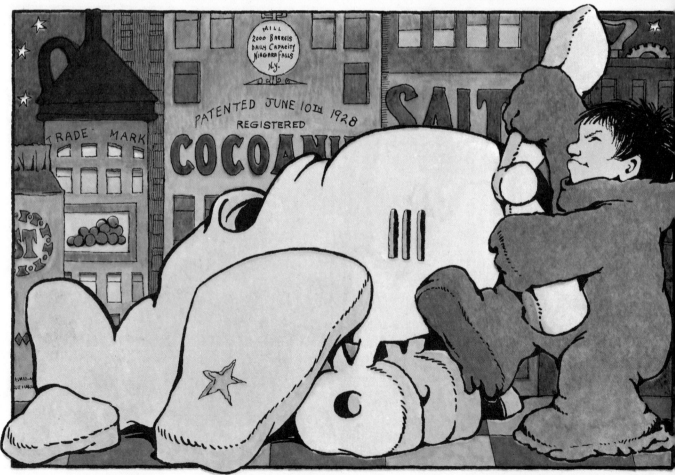

WHEN THE BAKERS RAN UP
WITH A MEASURING CUP, HOWLING:

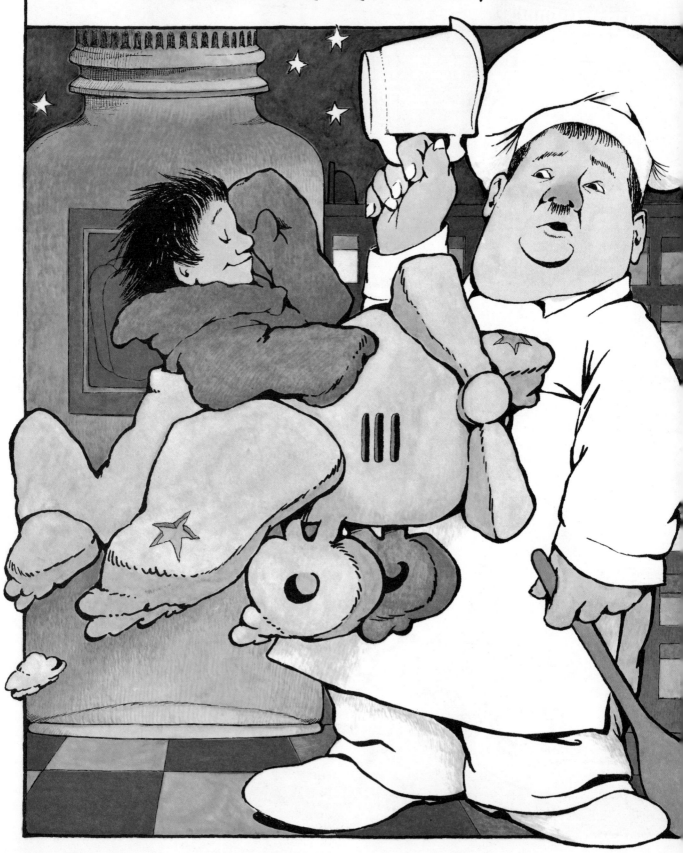

SO THE BAKERS THEY MIXED IT AND BEAT IT AND BAKED IT.

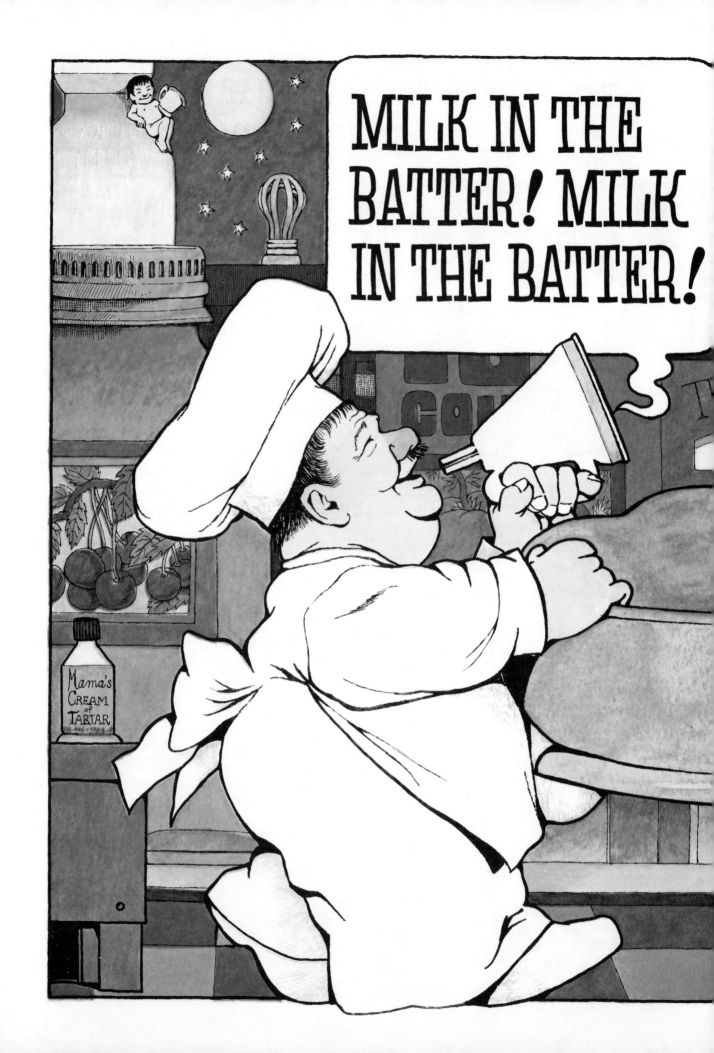